Table of Contents

Publisher's Notes

Disclaimer

This publication is intended to provide helpful and informative material. It is not intended to diagnose, treat, cure, or prevent any health problem or condition, nor is intended to replace the advice of a physician. No action should be taken solely on the contents of this book. Always consult your physician or qualified health-care professional on any matters regarding your health and before adopting any suggestions in this book or drawing inferences from it.

The author and publisher specifically disclaim all responsibility for any liability, loss or risk, personal or otherwise, which is incurred as a consequence, directly or indirectly, from the use or application of any contents of this book.

Any and all product names referenced within this book are the trademarks of their respective owners. None of these owners have sponsored, authorized, endorsed, or approved this book.

Always read all information provided by the manufacturers' product labels before using their products. The author and publisher are not responsible for claims made by manufacturers.

Print Edition 2014

The Sissy Series: Taboo Erotica Volume 2

Sissy Erotica - Four Short Stories

Howie Hayes

Book 1: Be Careful What You Wish For

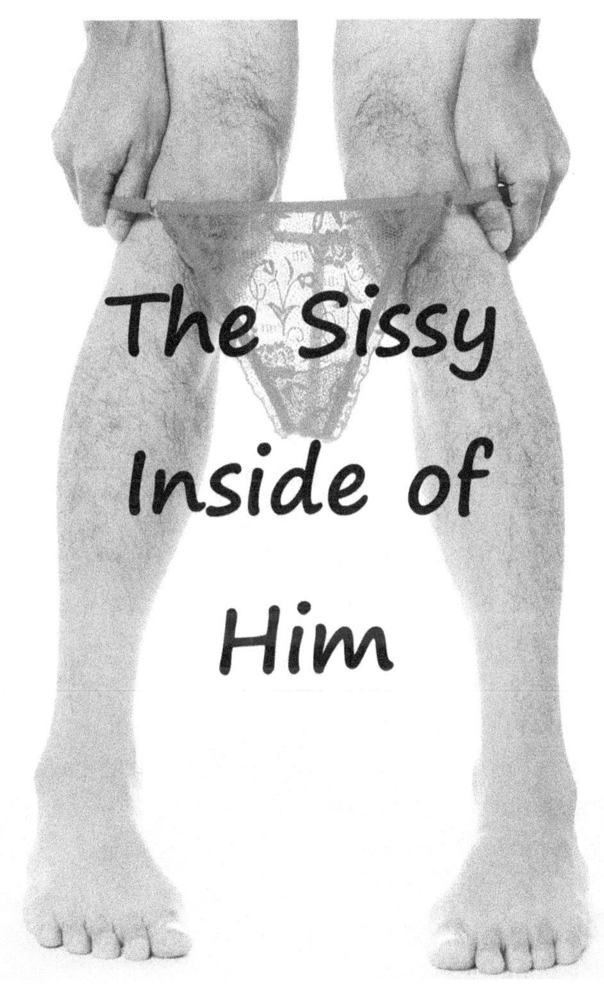

He wasn't supposed to be here, well not like this anyway, completely hard and with a line of sweat that ran down his forehead, half nervous, half incredibly turned on. If Melanie ever caught him like this, there would be no lying about it. The lingerie store was far too great a temptation to walk away though.

In the back were the bins full of panties. Tiny lace G-strings, silky thongs and then his favorite, the full cut, satin ones, just feeling the material on his fingertips made him shiver and if he'd been alone here, he would let out the moan that he felt rising up in his chest. He was too far gone and grabbed half a dozen pairs of the underwear, in a variety of colors and forced himself to quickly walk to the cashier.

"Do you want a gift receipt?" the tall, thin blond at the register asked him.

"What?" he could hardly breathe, let alone speak. "No, that's fine," he was fumbling, his palms were damp and he couldn't pull the wallet out of his back pocket.

"What if your wife needs to return them?" she wouldn't leave him alone and he wanted to scream.

"It's fine, what's the total?" his pulse raced in his neck, the throbbing beat at his temple made everything else pale by comparison. He had to leave.

Finally, with his bag of forbidden treasures, he made it to the car. He was breathing so hard that he felt as if he'd run a mile, but it was like this every time. When he opened the bag and ran his hand through the pile of panties, he smiled and the wet spot in his underwear seeped through to the crotch of his pants.

The cell phone disrupted his slow, dirty daydream; it was his wife was calling to give him more directions. "Matt, when are you coming home?"

His voice was hoarse when he spoke, his hand still fingering the panties and his erection beyond his control, "Soon, honey. Do you need anything?" he went through the usual routine.

"No, I'll see you when you get here. Love you," when she

would say that, especially at moments like this, the guilt would rush back and he imagined coming clean and telling her everything and the words would be right there, on the tip of his tongue, but instead he just said the usual good-byes and hung up quickly before he did anything stupid.

She would never understand.

That night, he held her until her gentle breathing had become rhythmic enough that he knew she'd never hear him leave. Matt eased his arm out from under her and stopped, watching her sleep. Melanie had gotten even more beautiful over the years, if that were possible. Her long, dark mane of curls spread out on the pillow beneath her, her full, pink lips that always looked as if she were ready to blow a kiss, her body may be softer now than it had been in college but her curves remained and it drove him crazy to watch her bottom bounce as she passed him.

If only that were enough. He shook his head to rid himself of the thought, he needed it and the need was powerful, palpable and after all, he'd been so good.

In the den, he found his hiding spot. In the corner, behind some shelves, where all the dirty, little secrets that he would come and visit lie in wait for his next slip, he retrieved the new bag of panties. His pajama pants came down quickly, he stood naked and his hard-on slapped against his pelvis as he pulled up the pink, silky panties that he had chosen for this evening. Matt knew which DVD he would watch and once he pressed play and sank back in the black, leather chair, he knew that it wouldn't be long.

The woman walked across the shabby motel room, she was dressed in a tight, black dress, the dark stockings ran up her slender legs and the high heels completed her outfit. Her ankles were unsteady in the shoes and you could see immediately that she was unaccustomed to stilettos. She sat down and her long, blond hair hung over one shoulder, she licked her red lips expectantly and a door that out of view opened.

The man stood at the foot of the bed and handed her the

crumpled bills, her hand was trembling as she slid the money into the handbag that she had placed on the mattress. When he unzipped his pants and produced the enormous cock, Matt started rubbing his shaft back and forth through the satin panties. The man grabbed the blond roughly by the shoulder and pushed her down on her knees, with the other hand; he rubbed the wide, throbbing head of his dick on her lips. She looked up, hungry and eager for all of it, and opened her mouth wide to take the thick shaft in her mouth. Matt's panties were soaked now as he watched, shivering and biting his lip to keep the moan inside.

The camera zoomed in on the woman, bobbing her head up and down to take more and more of the monstrous penis that fucked her red mouth. A dribble of her saliva trickled down and hung from her bottom lip and Matt knew it would only be another minute or two before he exploded. The blond pulled up the bottom of the dress, drug it up over her hips and her small bulge in the red bikini panties she wore was exposed. She rubbed herself in her panties, the front of the material soaked with her sissy cream; she touched herself while servicing the man on her knees.

Matt felt his dick jolt and his orgasm shot out, coating the inside of his slick underwear, he gripped his shaft and felt wave after wave of his hot load cover him and the moan he'd been holding back for so long finally erupted from his throat.

"That's interesting, Matt," Melanie's voice, hard as glass, cut through the air and his hard-on withered as his heart sank. There was nowhere to go and no way he could hide it, he turned the chair around slowly and felt his cheeks burn and his stomach lurch. He couldn't meet her stone, cold gaze.

Melanie walked toward him, silent as she crossed the carpet, he should have known that she would catch him, she'd always been smarter than him. When she reached his desk, she looked at the movie on the screen, which had continued to play and she watched as the blond held her tongue out to catch the long spurts of the man's orgasm, her red lipstick smudged and her chin dripping with cum.

She looked down and saw his ruined panties, he realized that his hand was still on his tiny, soft penis and tore it away, hoping she hadn't noticed.

"So this is what you do in here, night after night, huh?" her lips pouted, her short tee-shirt barely covered her bottom and if he hadn't just came all over himself, he'd grab her right now and reach for her round cheeks. "Do you want to say anything to me?" and he swallowed hard, trying to form the words, even more nervous now that she was so close.

Matt could only mumble something unintelligible.

"I see," Melanie shot one eyebrow up and her round upper lip became a sneer, "Well, be careful what you wish for."

She left him to his imagination and he didn't dare return to their bed. After he had cleaned up and threw the shameful panties away, he tossed from one side to the other on the couch, picturing what she would do next. In the morning, his back hurt and his heart ached, he noticed the puffy, purple circles under his eyes and when he saw her in the kitchen with her coffee, he didn't understand how she could look so beautiful. Her long hair was up and two perfect ringlets caressed her neck, the fitted, dark blue dress hugged her curves and her face glowed.

She never smiled but before she left for the day she told him, "Be home at six o'clock tonight," and her shoes tapped to the door without another word.

Matt spent the day checking his phone for a sign of her, flashing back to the movie and the panties and nervously watched the time, which had never passed more slowly. When he arrived at the house, five minutes early, he called out to her, "Honey? Where are you?"

"Up here," she answered and he felt a glimmer of hope as he made his way up carefully, step by step. She didn't sound angry and he wondered if she weren't in the bedroom, wearing lingerie of her own, waiting to take him into her arms.

There was no sign of her on the bed, he walked through the closet and opened the bathroom door. Melanie sat on the edge of the large, sunken tub and waved to him, "Come here, Matt," and his heart hammered in his chest as he reached her, trying to press his lips to her but she evaded his grasp.

Melanie loosened his tie and unbuttoned his shirt, whisking the clothes off and when she grabbed his belt buckle to pull it loose, he murmured, "Oh baby, I want you so much," and the goosebumps that started at his neck ran down to the back of his thighs as he felt her fingers along his bare skin. He was standing at attention for her once he was naked, his dick waved to her and he longed for her touch.

"Get in the tub," she told him and he did as she directed, hoping that her blue dress would come off, over her head and he'd feel her legs open as she slid on top of him, he'd hold her bottom in his hands while she fucked him in the water.

She was silent and let him soak while she rummaged in the cabinets. Returning with a razor and shaving cream, she said, "sit up," and rubbed a dollop of the cream on his chest.

"Melanie, what are you doing?" he suddenly realized that she still hadn't smiled and the suspense was killing him.

"Shaving you," her voice was flat, she didn't care to elaborate.

"Wait," he tried to move, avoid the pink razor that was about to slide down the center of the white goo and remove his hair. "What's going on, honey?"

"Well, Matt, as I see it," and it was too late, she had already taken two long strokes across his chest, "you want to be a girl," and he forgot to try and stop her, his heart was in his throat again as her hands passed back and forth over his skin, "a girl in a dress, wearing panties and sucking cock, right?" Melanie moved her hand lower to the top of his belly and he felt the razor scrape across his skin there as well. "First thing a girl has to do is shave."

She was halfway done with his belly before he could find

his voice. "Melanie, I don't want to be a girl, it's," his voice trembled but he pushed out the rest of it quickly, "it's just something I masturbate to sometimes."

"Bullshit, Matt," she was almost finished and he was hairless from neck to stomach. "Give me your arm," she sprayed more shaving cream and continued working the razor along every inch. "I've known for a long time what you really were, but I chose to go along with your little game."

Matt grabbed her forearm with one wet hand, "what am I?"

She finally looked him in the eye and a cold, wide smile spread across her face as she answered, "a little, sissy girl."

Melanie continued to shave and Matt trembled now under her touch, he was ashamed that his small dick bobbed up from under the water, as if it knew better than he the truth of what she said.

He complied when she told him to stand up and he looked down and watched her shave his legs. He couldn't help but let out a sigh when she reached his ball sack, a trickle of precum bubbled from his slit and slid down the length of him and puddled on her hand. "Don't you dare get your nasty sissy cream on me," her voice was as sharp as the razor. She raised her hand to his face and demanded, "Clean that up."

Matt shook his head no and felt Melanie's sharp nails dig into his chin as she forced him down, "don't you ever tell me no, sissy."

He obeyed and tasted himself on her hand, the little salty droplets dissolved on his tongue and he couldn't deny that he felt more like the girl in the movie already. He closed his eyes and opened his mouth and in his mind's eye, the images of her sliding to her knees rolled by slowly, Melanie interrupted him with an audible click of her tongue.

"What did I tell you?" She smirked and jerked his dick in this direction and that direction while she removed every last piece of hair. When she was finished, she told him to bend over and put his ass up in the air. Matt clenched and heard the groan that came from him as his beautiful wife ran her hands over his cheeks, then up to his crack, it was a dreadful combination of lust and fear when the razor blade moved along the tender, pink skin around his asshole.

"There you go, much better," she was finished and rinsing off the pink razor. "Rinse off," she told him and he sank back into the water, grateful that he could try to hide his erection again.

Melanie let the water out of the tub and handed him a towel to dry. "You'll need lotion, sissy, to keep your skin silky smooth," and she opened a tub with a pink lid, scooped up a hand of the perfumed cream and slowly slid her hands from his neck down his back. Matt melted under her touch and hoped that this was the last of it. After she rubbed his body, she'd take pity on him and take him by the hand and walk him to the bedroom where he could show her what a man he still was.

His hand trembled in hers as she led him out of the bathroom, through the closet once more and gently guided him to the bed. "Baby, I love you so much," he reached behind her to press his hands to the soft, sloping curve of her cheeks, if she would stay there, standing between his legs, he'd push the dress up and feel her bare bottom that bounced beneath the lace of her panties.

"You're not done yet, sissy," she dismissed him with a look and walked back to the closet. She approached him with a handful of lace and satin. "It's better to put the garter belt and stockings on first," Melanie pulled him up and before he understood what she was doing, she had hooked the back of the white, lace garter belt behind him. It was snug on his hips and when he looked down; he saw the white ribbons with the tiny, pink flower bows that dangled and brushed against his legs. At the sight of what he was wearing, large drops of precum oozed down his thigh.

"Thought you'd like that, sissy," she looked up for a moment and rolled her eyes at him. The sheer, white stockings had seams up the back and she started pulling one up his leg. Matt could hardly breathe as he saw the silky material rise up on his thigh, the top edge of the lace was snug on his skin and when she fastened the stockings to the garter belt, he hadn't meant to say a word but he whispered, "oh God."

"Now for your favorite part," she stayed on the carpet and grabbed a pair of white, see-through panties, "put these on," she said as she helped guide them up his long legs. When he felt her tuck his dribbling penis into the front of the soft material, he grabbed her hand as if to keep her there.

"Please, Melanie," he didn't know what he was begging for, did he want her to stop or finish his transformation?

"Don't get grabby," she freed herself easily, his grasp was getting weaker the more feminine she made him. "Let me help you with the bra," she rose up and turned him around to place the matching sheer fabric over his hard nipples and hook him from behind. When she brought him back to face her, she couldn't help but giggle when she touched one of his pink, pointy buds, then jiggled his flesh, "you almost have little titties!" she exclaimed.

"Now sit down," she had walked back to the bathroom and spoke to him through the door, "you need help with your face."

It was no longer a turn-on and his pulse raced and his dick drooped instantly. "What do you mean?" his voice sounded higher as well.

She returned with a bag of brushes and containers, "Your make-up, what did you think?" she shrugged her shoulders as if this had happened a thousand times before.

"Wait," Matt put his hand up, seeing it tremble, he put it down quickly but continued his protest, "this has gone far enough. Come on, I know you're mad, but no make-up."

Melanie's hands were on her hips and she shook her head. "Don't you remember what I said, Matt?" the brush touched his cheeks and she swirled it around in a container of pink before she twirled it on his skin once more. "Be careful what you wish for."

He whined and hung his head, all of the fight had left him and he felt limp, she turned his face, touched him here, told him which way to look and to pucker his lips. She stood up, and with a look of satisfaction, rubbed her hands together. "Looking good," she said more to herself than him and walked away once more, returning with a long, blond wig.

"This is going to be perfect on you," Melanie pulled the wig over his head and tucked his hair in underneath. "You're going to adorable for company."

Matt slipped back to the scene in the movie that he had jerked off to so many times before that he knew every second, every move, and every sigh. He had pictured himself taking her place over and over while touching himself in the damp panties, but now, the image frightened him.

"Company?" it was the only word that came out and he didn't understand why he asked in a high, girlish pitch.

"Of course, Matt, we're having some guests over," she was walking back and forth from the closet to the bed. "I have to pull this dress on over your hips, don't want to mess up your hair, girl," and there was nothing to do but comply, giving her his feet, watching the pink material glide up over his stockings cover the panties, up to his bra and then she zipped him quickly inside.

"You're going to have to practice a little to walk in these," she warned Matt, holding the hot pink high heels in front of her, "and I want you to impress him." The word him sent a new wave of fear through his body, and he jammed his feet into the shoes.

"Who is "him"?" he meant to shout but it just came out in a pathetic whimper.

"Just look at yourself in the mirror," Melanie stood to the side, and gestured to the full-length mirror that hung on the back of the closet door. Matt walked with tiny steps, trying to keep his ankles straight, finally he arrived and he was mesmerized by the beautiful woman that stared back at him. The blond curls touched his shoulders and the dress pressed against his small breasts, the curve of his new hips enticed him and his legs shimmered in the white stockings. He puckered his pink, shiny lips and the girl blew him a kiss. She winked and twirled her hair like the coquette that she had always been. She shimmied when she walked and after a few minutes of practice, she could twirl, the hem of the pink dress fluttering around her thighs.

"I told you that you'd look beautiful, sissy," Melanie touched his shoulder and suddenly he was her husband again and puckered his lips in her direction, wanting nothing more than to feel her round mouth on him and melt in her arms.

"Yeah," she grimaced and pulled away, "save that for our guest." The doorbell rang at that moment and she called over her shoulder as she made her way out the door, "you wait there, sissy, the stairs are too much for you."

Matt sank to the bed, and strained to listen to the voices, Melanie laughed, a low voice chuckled, his heart beat so loud in his ears that he couldn't catch the words. Sweat snaked down the back of his neck and he felt it dribble on his long, blond hair and dripped down into his dress. Every footstep that he heard coming back up the stairs seemed to echo in his chest.

Melanie opened the bedroom door and peeked at him, "Richard, I'd like you to meet Maddie!" she made the introductions with a smile on her face. The man that walked in behind her was taller than Matt by at least six inches, even if Matt had stood in the heels, he would look down on his blond head. He strode briskly and reached the bed, Matt saw that his chest was far wider, his neck thicker, his hands looked as if they could break him in two easily if he but chose.

"Maddie," he nodded to the girl on the bed before sitting down, his massive thigh touching Matt's, sending fingers of sensation, something hot was running along his leg and up to the small, pink bit of flesh that simmered in the silky panties. "Melanie tells me that you have never sucked a dick before."

"But that she's always wanted to, isn't that right, sissy girl?"

his wife stood in the corner and finished the sentence.

Matt could only shake his head yes.

"Well, Maddie, is that true?" Richard's large paw was on the girl's knee, and then slowly moved back and forth on the soft stockings, up a little higher, almost reaching under the hem of her dress. "Are you a virgin, little girl?"

Without thinking about it, Maddie spoke for him. "Yes," she cooed and batted her eyelashes at the handsome man who was touching her.

"That's so hot," he said as his wide palm reached up, over her little belly, to her right breast, skimming over the fabric of the dress and sending a long, hot ache down the entire length of her body. "Are you ready to show me how much you want to suck my cock, sissy girl?" he asked and his hand held her chin so that Maddie had no choice but to look him in the eye.

"Yes," she whispered and slowly, she moved off the bed and dropped to her knees, in a way that seemed strangely familiar and waited as the tall man unbuckled and unzipped, his pants made a jangle as they dropped to his ankles. Maddie could see the tip of his cock bulging above the waistband of his underwear and the clear outline of the solid, meaty shaft still hidden. She licked her lips and reached her hand up to touch him.

"Do you like touching that big, hard cock?" the man pressed her small hand to his erection and moved it up and down.

"Oh yes," she couldn't take her eyes off it and felt a throb in her own wet panties.

"Take it out for me then, sissy," he told her, his voice was low and authoritative and Maddie instinctively knew he must be obeyed.

She pulled down the underwear with both hands and gasped when she saw the long, pink dick, it was enormous and too wide for her to hold with one hand.

"What do you want to do with that cock, Maddie?" it was a rhetorical question, her mouth was wide open, she held it by the base with two hands and she felt the drool drop down her bottom lip and slide down her chin.

"Suck it," her whole body was shaking as she confessed.

"You know why you want to suck that cock, sissy?" he forced the girl to look up, his strong hand lifting her face once more, "Because that's all a sissy is good for. Now show me how you respect a real man," and he moved his hand off of her chin and reached around the back of her head to push her down to take the throbbing dick inside.

Maddie touched the tip of her tongue to lap the head of his cock, licking up his salty liquid that oozed there, then moved down to run her mouth around the ridge of his bulbous head. She felt him pulse in her two hands and with a whimper, closed her mouth around the head and swirled her tongue slowly, tasting him between her lips.

"That's it sissy, open your mouth and take it all," he commanded and she knew that the alpha male must be obeyed. She puffed her cheeks out and moved her head back and forth to take another inch and then another of the handsome man's solid erection. Soon she had half of the thick penis in her mouth and when she realized that she was only halfway there and the head of his cock touched the back of her mouth already, a splatter of her sissy cream soaked the front of her panties.

She was going to be absolutely stuffed with cock. Relaxing her mouth, she plunged ahead and took him inside deeper and deeper, until Maddie felt his slick head in her throat. She couldn't spread her lips any wider and she worked them up and down there, she was almost to the root and she gagged a little, a wet line of her spit wet her chin.

"Take your hands off now sissy, only use your mouth," he must be obeyed and she placed her small hands on his inner thighs now and the feel of his skin on her made the wet spot on her white panties even bigger. She started sucking him faster, her head bobbed as she had seen the woman on the movie do, the sound of her wet sissy hole being stuffed and released, just to be stuffed even wider with cock made her pick up the tempo.

"That's it, sissy, suck that cock like you were made to do," he man's hands on her head weren't even necessary, she wouldn't dream of stopping now until she swallowed his load. Her tongue lashed up and down and soaked him and teased him, she licked every ridge, the veiny line, she sucked him down to the tips of his bush of pubic hair and back up to his thick head.

The man started to pant and his hips thrust up, off the bed, driving into her mouth, he fucked her face, in deeper than before and back out until her greedy little mouth reached forward to take him back inside. Maddie could feel the tremor that ran down the length of him and she knew that in a moment, he would fill her to the brim with his buttery jizz.

She rammed her head down so that she would feel the first shot course down her throat. He howled as he spurt, shoving the salty mouthful deep inside. Maddie moved her head back to taste the next spasm on her tongue, feeling his sticky juices cover her there, she swallowed and when her lips were closed he coated her lip sticked mouth with another dollop of creamy semen. Maddie licked it up and kept her mouth open as the rest of waves left him and slapped her chin, her lips, her cheek and finally felt him weave his hand through her hair once more as he told her, "clean me up, sissy."

Maddie sucked up every last drop, lapping at his head again and tasting his slit, she licked around the head once more and then dropped her face in his lap, her breath coming fast and her entire body on fire with her girlish want. Melanie reappeared from the corner and now spoke to the man. "Did she do a good job, Richard?"

"Oh yes," he patted her head, the wig moved under his touch. "Maddie knows her place very well."

"Good sissy," Melanie touched her arm and when Maddie looked up and saw her pouty lips curl into a smile, Matt tried to speak.

"You wait there, Maddie, while I walk our guest out," she told him and once they were gone, Matt looked in the mirror and watched as he took off the wig and wiped his ruined lipstick off. He slid out of the heels and unzipped the dress with the damp place where his dick had leaked. He was attempting to remove the bra when Melanie returned.

"What are you doing?" she was shocked and rushed over to pick up the dress and shake it out. "You're not done, we've got to fix your hair," she leaned in to inspect his white encrusted lips, and wash the cum off your face.

"What's happening now?" all Matt wanted to do was take her in his arms and feel her chest to chest and feel her velvet lips on his neck, her soft kisses up to his ear and then feel her under him, wet and ready for him.

"We have several guests coming tonight, Matt," she had reverted back to his name and suddenly he could taste the load of sperm that rose up in his throat. "I hope you enjoy it," she licked her round, bottom lip once and then smiled, "I know I will."

BOOK 2: THE SISSY COP AND THE SUSPECT

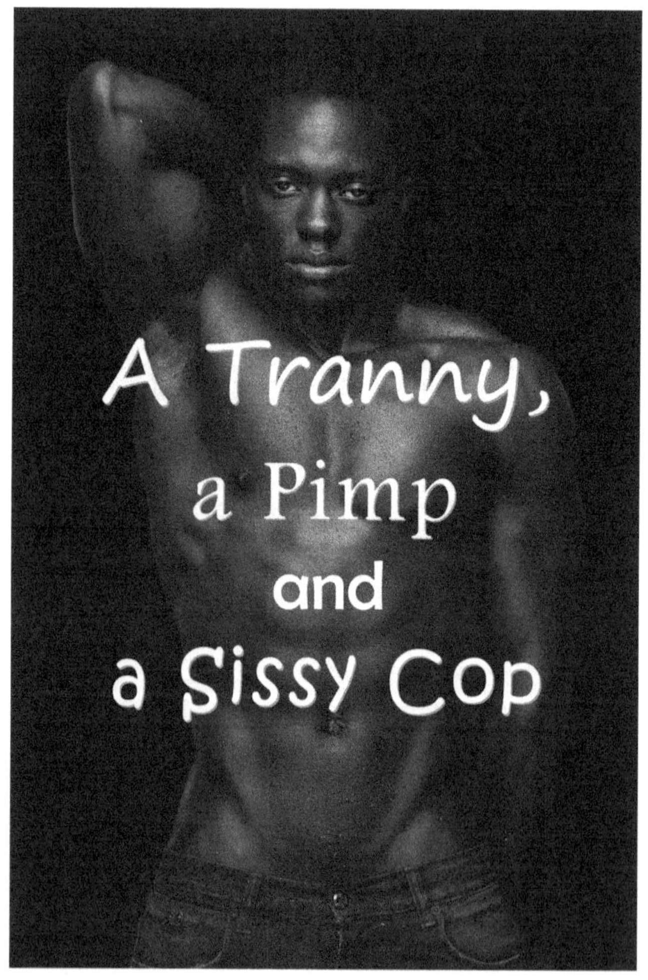

Very few things rattled him, being his height and his size, usually he was the one who inspired fear, or at least intimidation, but he felt the chill creep down between his shoulder blades when he first saw her and it had never really faded.

As he made his way to the room, he recalled their first meeting; she sat in silence in the metal chair, hands cuffed to the desk in front of her as she waited. It had been a long night and she had been frisked, fingerprinted, tossed in a cell and had spent more than an hour in the interrogation room, with no clock, time stood still. Yet, when he opened the door, she had clearly been in charge from the beginning. Her red, full lips curled into a familiar smile as she asked him for a cigarette.

"There's no smoking in here, ma'am," he stared at her legs as he made his way to the chair on the opposite side of the table. Legs for miles, milky-white, curvy calves wrapped in black fishnet stockings, her dress was so short that he could see the lace band at the top, hugging an elegant thigh. She clicked her black heels on the worn tile and returned his gaze when he sat down.

Her long, red nails pointed at him as she attempted to raise her hands, "then how about if you take these off?" her husky voice was like a tongue in his ear.

"Sorry," he shook his head no, shrugging his wide, solid shoulders, "can't do that. I'd like to ask you some questions," he cleared his throat and shuffled with papers and pretended that her cleavage wasn't exposed and the lace at the top of the bra wasn't tempting him to sit up and take notice.

"Yes, I'm single," she batted her eyelashes at him and whipped the long, red curls back over her shoulder, her hands continued to plead with him for release, but the rest of her body knew the kind of power she had.

"This is serious," he scowled at her, clicking the pen in his huge paw, the other hand wandered out of eyesight and adjusted his pulsating hard-on that was making it impossible to see the boxes and lines on the form. No wonder the officers had left her handcuffed, she radiated sex appeal like a perfume and it threatened to overpower him.

He read through the form and she answered every question, the knowing smile had never left her face, as if she knew that in his mind's eye, she was uncuffed and her dress was up over her hips and her full, round ass was pressed against the table while his strong hands kneaded the flesh of her upper thighs and his lips explored every nook and crevice. At the end of the interview, he had cordially unlocked the cuffs and stood to walk her out.

The red-head's eyes traveled his body and he felt her study the bulge that had continued throughout their talk and was now making a puddle of want at the front of his uniform. "You're a big boy," she murmured before swiping her tongue across her top lip, leaving her mouth wet-looking and in need of nibbling.

His face was warm and although he knew that she couldn't see him blush, his chocolate skin would prevent that, she obviously noticed that he was tongue-tied. The hard-on never left as he walked her to the front door, watching the band at the top of the stockings as she sashayed through the throng of people, dismissing every smile and every turned head as she passed, her bottom bouncing in the impossibly short dress with every step. He was mesmerized and could only offer her his card between two trembling fingers before she left, "if you think of anything, please call me, Miss."

She took his card and turned, offering her hand and he was barely able to ignore his impulse to kiss it rather than shake it, he wanted to draw her palm up to his mouth and let his lips wander up her wrist, up the pale, delicate skin to her bare shoulder before running his teeth up her neck. "That's Miss Vivian," she flashed her teeth at him as if to tell him that she knew about the biting, she read the card, repeating his name, "Officer Robert Jefferson," she winked and he felt the need to steady himself. "Yes, I just might call you," and with one last toss of her fiery, red curls, she left him, shaken and unable to forget her.

Then out of the blue, she had called and he knew it was her, her voice caressed him like a hand in his hair, like fingers unbuttoning his collar, she only had to say, "Robert? This is Miss Vivian, how are you?" for it all to come rushing back.

Now he was making his way to her, down the hallway of doors, this place was known for drug deals and violent encounters with pimps and johns and the wallpaper hung and bubbled and peeled back to reveal mold and bugs that scurried back to the corners where they came from. He had been here many times before, always in an official capacity until today.

He knocked at her door, Room 223 and noticed the indentation on his third finger of his left hand where he had slid the ring off, he patted his pants pocket to make sure he still felt its outline there. The guilt of not wearing it was only second to the desire he had for her.

"Come in, Robert," she stood in the doorway and beckoned for him to enter, one arm up, the other on her hip, the tight green dress she was wearing skimmed every delicious curve and when she walked to the mattress, he thought she undulated like a snake. "Sit down, make yourself comfortable," her nails were inky, black now as she patted the place next to her and flashed him a smile.

He made a noise as he sank down beside her, the bed creaking under his weight and then suddenly she was in his arms, so small, pressed up against his chest, his hands melted down her back to her ass as he held her tightly to him and moaned as he opened his mouth to kiss her.

Her lips were hot and fit his and her tongue was wet satin that slid along his, she returned every dart forward and allowed him all the way inside her mouth, smelling her, tasting her, exploring her, it was as if he had just discovered that he was starving and she was a necessity. He could hear the slippery sounds of their kiss as it continued and nothing else and he wondered how many times over the last few days he had been right here, in his mind, on top of her, on her bed, his mouth devouring her.

When she withdrew, Robert contented himself by grazing her round, bottom lip with his teeth and feeling her pant under him, "you wanted to do that for a while, haven't you?" she asked, it was a rhetorical question, of course she knew.

He answered by sliding his lips down her neck and rubbing his face in the red curls, her perfume and her body heat rose up and combined into something intoxicating that drug him down her throat and to her shoulders, he was gulping for air by the time he found his lips at her décolletage and he stopped himself there. He had to take the dress off.

Robert slid his fingers under the straps at her shoulders and worked the green fabric down until her small, pale breasts were bare and he felt the tremor run down his back as he saw the small, pink stone nipples, pointed, ripe and ready for his tongue.

"Yes, do it," she knew that he longed to bury his face there, holding her breasts together, feeling the soft curves in his large hands as he lapped and nibbled at one nipple and then the other, wetting her skin and sucking along the underneath, tasting her everywhere and listening to her low whimper and her whispered request for more. Vivian arched her back to feed him her flesh and he felt her hips grinding into him, making his erection swell and leak in his pants.

"God, I want you so much," his confession was pointless, she could feel his cock rubbing against her urgently but he felt that she should know about the sleepless nights since they met where he had laid on the couch and stared at the ceiling, seeing only her lips and her long legs walking away. He couldn't wait anymore and his bulky body started to make its way down on the mattress, he heard the squeak of springs as he grabbed the dress and pulled it from her slender frame, down the long legs that he'd seen around his shoulders a thousand times, tossing it aside. He was on his knees between her legs, which was exactly where he longed to be.

Robert's lips touched the flesh-colored band at the top of her thigh-highs, his tongue pushing up the pink strap of the garter belt and meandering up to the solid band of lace that hooked around the curve of her hips. He could feel her trembling below him, her skin was on fire everywhere he touched her and when he parted the slit of her rose-colored crotch less panties, her pink cock was unleashed and the shaft bobbed and the wet tip touched his lip. "What a sweet boy," she murmured, her dainty fingers wrapped in his hair and her nails tracing up his neck, she was pushing his mouth down to her beautiful dick, knowing it was completely unnecessary, there was nothing more that he wanted than to fill his mouth with every bit of her satiny skin.

He ran his tongue through the puddle of clear liquid that lie on her pelvis and shuddered before wrapping his hand around the base of her cock and caressing the wide, pulsing head of her erection and licking up her essence that ran from her slit. He pushed the tip inside, drinking her juices, feeling her sweetness coat his tongue and melt down his throat before licking her softly under the ridge beneath the tip. She moaned and he looked up to see her eyes on him, half-closed and hazy with want, she raised her hips and he heard her say yes as he opened his mouth to take her shaft inside.

His tongue touched her skin all the way down and all the way back up, she thrust when he reached the bottom, his hands now clutching the flesh of her inner thighs, it was only his mouth on her now and he gave her all of it. Robert felt the head of her cock touch the top of his throat with each bob of his head and drew her in further as his lips clamped around her hot skin.

"Oh, that's so good, just like that," her hands caressed his head and drew him near, her slender hips writhed as she drove in and out of his mouth, fucking him harder and faster now, feeding him every inch of the cock he craved, Robert's fingers fluttered across the tip of his own bulge that ached for attention, simmering away in his wet underwear. His groan was muffled on her cock and he took his hand away, afraid that even another minute and he'd burst.

Her body rocked against the bed and she called out to him, "I'm going to cum so hard, all the way down your throat," her voice was throaty and then came a soft cry as the first spasm ran down her legs and she spurted a long, hot dash of her sweet, salty cum down his throat.

Robert pulled his head back to feel the next squirt on his tongue and let it trickle down and coat his insides, marking him as hers, again and again, she pushed every last drop out and watched him take it from her, sliding his mouth up to drink the droplets from her slit once more as he felt her shiver under him with delight.

He didn't know how long they stayed like that, time stood still as she dripped inside him and he was on his knees, continuing his slow, gentle worship, her hands on his neck, her moans in his ear, it wasn't until she spoke that he fell out of his daydream. "Are you ready, Robert?" she asked quietly.

"Yes, Miss Vivian," he let her flesh fall from his lips as he answered and nodded in agreement.

She sat up and her angelic expression had disappeared, it had been replaced by a smirk, her lip curled as she grabbed his chin and she looked him in the eye with wicked glee, "I don't think you know what you've asked for," were the last words that he heard before the knock on the door interrupted them.

"Hey, baby," she said when she answered the door and Robert didn't see who entered, on his knees, his head pressed against the damp place on the mattress where her scent marked the sheet, but he heard the footsteps approach him. "He wants to be your slut too, baby," her voice was a tease now and it was all for him, the other man, the one who was sitting on the bed now and gripping him by the shoulder as Robert turned his head to see her pimp.

"Is that so?" the man in the suit asked, his bony fingers digging into his flesh, the man had a predatory look and his eyes were studying every inch of him, his uniform, his face, Robert imagined that he even saw the look of desire that was still imprinted on his face. "You know what's involved, bitch? You are going to have to be trained, you know that?" and Robert bowed his head, determined to do whatever was required for her.

"Yes, sir," he murmured, turning to stare at the woman in pink and feel the want surging through his body once more.

"Get him undressed," the pimp snapped at Vivian and Robert wanted to rise and hold out his bulging bicep to protect her, but a glance from her was enough to keep him in place.

Vivian's soft fingers unbuttoned the front of his shirt and he closed his eyes as the pleasure coursed through him, her skin on his skin, her hands sliding over his muscles, sending a thrill through every nerve, he felt her pull the shirt off his arms and the fingernails scratching down his back.

She unbuckled his belt and pulled the heavy, leather strap from his waist, "get up, Robert," she prompted him and he felt his thighs shake as she pulled his pants down. Removing his shoes, in a moment or two, he was bent over and clutching the sticky sheets, cheeks exposed and teeth clenched.

"Now you have the right to remain silent, bitch," the man grabbed him by the back of the head and shoved a rubber ball in his mouth. Robert grunted when he felt the strap buckle at the nape of his neck, it was tight enough that every breath was sharp. "V, grab his wrists," Robert felt her delicate hands wrap around his skin, soft and rough at the same time, he let her hold his hands behind his back while the metal clicked and then clicked again. The man had handcuffed him with his own cuffs and he couldn't even scream for release.

"Help him on the bed, V," the man snapped at her, Robert continued to tremble every time the pimp addressed her, he assumed that V was a name that the man had given her, as if she were his property and she weren't actually a goddess. On his knees, face to the bed, hands locked behind him, Robert was about to discover what the pimp had in mind to open him up.

"Oh yeah, look at that big dick," the man slid a long, cool

pole between Robert's thighs and he shivered at the touch of his nightstick running back and forth slowly on the back of his legs, grazing his heavy ball sack, a soft touch down his shaft and then back up, between his cheeks to touch the pink, puckered skin that ran down his crack. "He's going to be very popular with our customers, V. You ready for some competition?" the pimp asked and didn't wait for her to respond, instead told her, "Get the lube."

He informed Robert, "I gotta get you greased up a little, can't be damaging the merchandise," and Robert closed his eyes tightly and shook his head no in silence as the wet dollop landed on his asshole. "This is going to hurt, cop," the man told him as the head of the pole was introduced.

Robert's scream went nowhere, the ball gag kept his howl inside and only saliva escaped his mouth as he was slowly opened with the wide head, the long pole began its thrust inside and Robert felt spread open, ripped wide apart and on fire. "Don't fight it, Robert," Vivian's sweet voice was a tender caress even out of view and once she stepped around and sat on the bed so that he could see her, he stopped gasping for breath and just stared. Her warmth entered him and he relaxed, allowing the pole to continue its steady insertion.

"That's right, just relax," she ran her fingers through his hair again, and the nightstick hit home, touching his prostate, sending a shiver of want all the way from the spot to his toes and he rested his forehead on her stockings, "you want to be the best cock whore you can be now, don't you?" her voice lilted and he shook his head yes and let it happen.

The man backed the stick out and pushed it in and then backed it out again slowly, teasing him, Robert felt the steady drip from the head of his cock, his desire pouring out of him and covering the sheet below, the rhythm was pushing him to move his hips in the man's time and give him everything he was demanding.

Vivian was reaching back and for a moment her palm caressed his sculpted abs and then wandered down his body to his throbbing erection, feeling how wet he was, she whispered, "oh I knew you would like that, that big, black pole inside you, popping your cherry, feel how hard you are," and her fingers grasped his aching cock and stroked him slowly, back and forth, just as the man was fucking him now, and Robert knew that she would draw the orgasm from him, it was entirely under her control. "You're even harder now than when you were sucking my cock, aren't you?" he shook his head yes, and took every thrust and every touch until he was on the edge of exploding in her soft hand. She released his dick and left him there, straining to cum but not allowed.

"He is going to love to take cock, isn't he?" the pimp asked, the nightstick was still now and the man directed him, "hold it there in your pussy, bitch," and Robert clenched his anus around the stick, straining to keep it on his g-spot, squeezing and dribbling, draining his liquid onto the bed and holding back his climax with much difficulty.

"Now let's see how stretched out that pussy is," the man uncuffed his hands first, they were no longer needed, Robert was a subjugated whore now, he held onto the sheet and continued to follow instructions, squeezing the stick inside and wetting the rubber ball with his tongue as he imagined sucking Vivian's beautiful dick once more.

"I've got to try this out, V," the pimp explained to her and Robert heard the jingle of a belt and then a zipper and felt the weight of the man as he made his way to his position, between Robert's tree trunk thighs, "see how much dick this little cunt can take."

The man entered him completely in one push and Robert still couldn't scream but his whole body shook from the sensation of being filled, forced, taken and the cock stayed in place now, as the stick had, "tighten up that pussy for me, bitch," he commanded and Robert felt the moan rise in his throat even though it was silent.

Vivian had moved on the bed and knelt before him now,

with a gentle touch, the gag was unbuckled and the wet ball made a loud, sucking noise as it was released from between his lips. Robert looked up to her face and saw that she was hard once more, the long, pink cock had risen up from its hiding place in the lacy panties and jolted and beckoned for his mouth once more, "your mouth is so good, Robert, I want you again," it was no request and Robert sighed, there was no question, he didn't need her to ask.

She wiped the head of her dick on his bottom lip and squeezed out another droplet or two on the tip of his tongue when he opened his mouth. "That sweet tongue," she hung her head back and Robert saw the toss of red curls slide back over her shoulders as she made her way inside.

Being fucked in both holes, Robert moved his head down on the cock that filled his mouth as the man pulled back and then took every inch of the man's dick inside as he moved his mouth up to her wet tip. Skewered and owned, he was a cock whore and he realized that he loved it, being used for her pleasure and even the pimp's, he was full of her taste and knew that he'd swallow another mouthful of her cream while his asshole was pumped full of the man's hot, sticky release.

"V, he's got such a tight pussy," the man was rocking him back and forth on the bed now, giving Robert his full weight with every thrust, his pelvis slamming into his cheeks, the head of his cock touching the place that made his body vibrate with every move. Robert moaned on the hard flesh in his mouth, his body convulsing with delight and he felt himself topple over, the orgasm ripped from his body.

He sucked her furiously while rivulets of his climax coursed through his cock and splattered the bed below. "Robert, yes, just like that," she was close as well and he came while he felt her tensing in his mouth, slipping from between his lips at the last minute before covering his face in a salty stream of her buttery load.

The man behind him thrust hard one last time and Robert

could feel the wet heat entering him, shot after shot, his face touched the bed and he moaned, knowing that he'd feel the man's cum run down his legs and cover his ass when the pimp was done marking him.

"Fuck, that was hot, I love a new whore, V," the man was done with him, slapped his cheek and let Robert collapse to the bed in a wet heat, covered in stickiness, every muscle quivered and his body was a pulsing sensation of desire.

The man was leaving and Robert heard him mumble something to Vivian before the door closed behind him. Her sashay back to the bed was much slower and he turned his head to watch her walk, her pale skin shone with sweat and to Robert, she seemed to sparkle.

"Was that everything you expected, Robert?" her pouty lips were bare of lipstick now and he liked them better that way.

He felt as if he were too exhausted to even speak but answered her with a nod and a quiet, "yes, Miss Vivian."

"Are you ready for another surprise then?" she traced one long nail down his cheek and as spent as he was, he felt the familiar pull, her skin on his, it would always be exhilarating.

"Yes, Miss Vivian," he loved her name and loved hearing himself say it as he did over and over in his mind while masturbating to her.

"Get dressed, Robert and then we'll talk," she stood up, all business now and he knew that his time with her had come to an end and that obsessing over the next time was just beginning.

He was dressed and his hair combed into place, face washed and he could still smell her all over his body, which he did with a smile, not wanting to ever lose the sweet reminder. Robert sat on the bed and watched her moving back and forth, small, perky breasts bouncing with every step, the stockings and garters still perfectly in place, her pink dick tucked back into its hiding place behind the lace. She ran her fingers through the wild, red curls and he watched them sink back down her back, touching her porcelain skin.

"You are going to need to come to work whenever he calls now, do you understand?" she wasn't looking at him as she spoke, continuing to pace back and forth like something caged and longing to be free.

"I'll do whatever you tell me to do Miss Vivian," it was true, he would.

"There's something else you need to know," she paused, pursed her lips and then continued the steady pace, "he has ways of making your life," she paused again and he saw the little shiver run down her back and he could only imagine what awful thing she was remembering, "he'll make your life miserable if you don't do what he tells you."

"What do you mean?" he suddenly realized that she was referring to him and not her.

"Let me show you," she went to the dresser and picked something up that had been out of view until now. A camera had been there all the while and she clicked a button twice with her long nail.

The whole thing was on video. Every minute since he had walked in the room and sunk to his knees to taste her, the man, the cuffs, Robert winced as he watched himself being penetrated with the stick at first and then giving in with wild abandon as he took both her dick and the pimps. His heart beat faster and faster and as he watched himself cumming harder than he ever had in his life, he knew what she meant.

"This was his idea?" his pulse raced and he could hear the blood rush to the vein that throbbed in his temple.

"Yes, he wanted to make sure you didn't do anything stupid," she shrugged as if no explanation was needed. He was, after all, a cop.

He was rising up off the bed, still trembling, but now it was in anger, "how could you do this to me?" his voice was hard and clipped and he hated himself for talking to her like that and just hated her all at the same time. "You can tell him that if he tries that blackmail with me, he'll be in jail. Tell him I dare him," his fist clenched and everything in him wanted to sink to his knees and beg, wondering if the man would really call his bluff.

Robert tried to speak and nothing else would come out but a long breath and he forced himself to turn and walk briskly to the door and shut it as hard as he could behind him. He was almost running down the hall and his mind was going even faster. His goddess had turned on him with a smile.

It had been two excruciating weeks. She had never called and his cell phone had been in his hand the entire time, he even clutched it under his pillow at night, his wife had never asked why and he never volunteered. He spent less and less time in the bed with her anyway, plunged back into his previous world of fantasy; he spent most of his nights on the couch, recalling every line, every curve, and every sound. He could almost feel his fingers running through her long, red curls.

This morning, he promised himself to stop. The pimp wasn't going to take any chances, but that didn't ease his heartache in the least. Vivian, his brain ached from saying her name again and again and it had been just as many times that he had lectured himself to let it go. She had been a mirage, it had been a mistake, he was a fool, and he'd chided himself again and again.

"Jefferson," his boss only addressed him by his last name, "you're up, got a suspect in Interrogation 2. Don't worry," the man slapped him on the shoulder as he passed, "it's just another hooker."

When he opened the door, the first sight of her gleaming red curls caught his eye and he wanted to run to her but seeing her hands chained to the table made him stop. She looked up and smiled, her eyes drawing him in, her pouty lips were round and warm and he felt his eyes rebel as the traveled the rest of her slender frame. Her legs crossed and she rattled her cuffs, "Officer, can you get me out of these, please?" her voice was warm honey in his ear.

He glanced down at the ring on his finger, back in the place that it belonged, burrowing into the ridge that had been there. He cleared his throat and proceeded in the proper manner to tell her no, she was to remain that way for the duration.

Sitting down, his hands on the table, her fingers burned when they touched his and it all came back in long sighs and fantasies whispered in an ear. He trembled as he reached for his keys, knowing he was back where he belonged, "yes, Miss Vivian," he replied.

BOOK 3: I'M NOT GAY

It had happened so long ago, but he had never forgotten a minute of it and he replayed the details over and over every time. It was exactly the same, on the bed next to his friend in their dorm room, the young man's hand had closed over his own and then he placed his palm on the erection that poked up out of the front of his shorts.

"Hey," he felt a tingle down his spine, he sounded as nervous as he felt, "what are you doing?" he had asked his friend.

"Relax, Sam," the look on his friend's face was a mix of ecstasy and triumph. "Just stroke me, just like that."

His friend was much stronger and as Sam had fought to free his hand, the young man easily kept him pinned and in place. He seemed to enjoy the fight as much as the caress. "I don't want to do this," Sam whined.

"Sure you do," he flipped the front of his shorts down with his other hand and freed his huge cock, slapping it into Sam's hand and continued his slow up and down stroke.

Sam couldn't speak as he looked at his friend's dick. He was drawn to it, so much longer and thicker than his own, a darker brown than the rest of his honey-colored skin, it moved in his hand and the full, round head dripped a thick line of precum, which was wetting Sam's hand.

"I always knew you were a cocksucker," his friend murmured, spreading his legs wide and settling into the steady rhythm of Sam's hand. His friend continued to hold him in place but it had almost become unnecessary. Sam jerked the big dick that barely fit in his hand, up to the wet hand, pushing down the foreskin to the base and back up again. "Now get your mouth down there," his friend growled.

Sam felt the panic return in a wave that gripped him. "I'm not gay," was the only response he could come up with.

"I know," his friend said, the strong paw now reaching around to his neck, pushing his face closer and closer to the enormous cock that his hand was gripping tightly. "You're a natural cocksucker though."

The precum touched Sam's upper lip and he didn't know why his tongue darted out to taste it, salty and sweet, it dissolved quickly in his mouth.

"I've never sucked cock," he whispered, but he couldn't stop looking at the rivulet of clear liquid that ran down the meaty shaft in his hand.

"Then get ready to drink a load of cum, little virgin," the young Hispanic man had driven his head down another inch and Sam couldn't move. There was no other choice than to open his mouth.

His friend groaned when Sam's tongue lapped the head of his penis, scooping up the shimmering droplets of his liquid desire that spit from the slit. Sam could feel the man's hand at the back of his head, pushing and pulling him by a handful of his blond hair, but by the time he had half of the large shaft in his mouth, it was hardly needed. He loved the earthy smell of the dick, the weight of it in his mouth; he loved working his tongue along every ridge, now he was determined to get every inch of it inside him, down to the ball sack.

Sam gagged a little when he moved forward, the solid head touching the top of his throat, but when he relaxed his opening; he could easily fit the entire dick in his mouth. He slathered the man with his spit, pulling the cock out with his hand and licking up and down the length of him, running the tip of his tongue around the ridge under the head. His friend was only rubbing his head now, no force at all and Sam groaned when he licked up the sweet precum directly from the tiny slit. Back down on the cock, he ran his tongue under his friend's foreskin and tasted the brine under the thick skin.

His friend kept talking, giving directions, telling him what Sam was. "You're such a faggot for sucking cock, I could tell the first time we met. White boys like you are so weak for a real man's cock. You crave it and now you'll need to suck it for the rest of your life. You'll pretend that you don't want it, but when you meet a real man, in your heart you'll want to get on your knees and take his cum. You're just a cock slave and a cum-bucket." He continued on and on and the words stirred something in Sam's mind that traveled directly to his dick.

As he continued to suck harder and harder, his cheeks puffed out and his soaking, wet mouth moving at a furious tempo, he knew he loved every taste of the dick that was fucking his face; he couldn't wait to feel his friend force feed his hot load down his throat.

The young man's balls were drawn up tight and he warned him, "I'm about to give you your prize cocksucker, your first mouthful of man spunk. I want you to swallow every last drop," and with a groan that came deep from his belly, his friend unleashed ropes of his heavy, buttery orgasm down in Sam's throat. He spurt again and then again, Sam swallowing all of it, he could feel the ooze running down his esophagus and into his stomach, all he could taste was his friend's salty essence. Sam continued to flick his tongue across the man's head, carefully cleaning the last drops and a deep sigh of contentment escaped his lips.

"You really loved drinking all that cum, didn't you cock slave?" his friend asked, knowing it was a rhetorical question.

Sam was deeply ashamed, even though his own dick, pitiful in comparison had risen and strained in his pants, hard and pulsing the whole time the beautiful dick had been inside him. "Yes," he barely whispered it.

"I didn't hear you," his friend was going to make him say it.

"Yes, you were right about me," Sam confessed. He had already asked himself if it was a onetime thing or if he would be allowed to worship here again.

"It's obvious," his friend said, "now I want you to get on your knees," the young man had rolled up on an elbow and was pointing to the floor.

Sam's legs trembled as he moved and dropped into the prone position, how much lower would he sink? His friend stood in front of him, his softer penis, still long and full and wet from base to tip with Sam's mouth, he pulled his foreskin back and shook his dick twice. "Open your mouth slave," and Sam did as he was told.

His friend's piss was warm and he didn't even think to protest, his friend explained his actions, "I'm marking my cum-bucket. When you're with me, all you'll drink is cum and piss and you will call me Master and always be ready with your mouth, do you understand?" he cut the stream of urine off with a squeeze.

Sam shook his head yes, his tongue still out, longing for more.

His friend laughed, "Look at you, can't get enough of anything that comes out of a real man's cock. That's enough for today cocksucker," and once he was tucked back in his shorts, his friend left Sam there, alone, on his knees, with his aching hard-on leaking into his wet underwear.

The rest of the semester, Sam's secret hunger for cock grew. When he was making love with his girlfriend, and most especially when he was alone and masturbating, in the back of his mind he was always on his knees receiving the glorious dick that he craved. He thought of other dicks in passing but he returned, faithfully, to his Master and drank from him whenever he was told.

Once the semester was over and he was switched to a new dorm, he only saw his friend pass by, always with a crowd and there was never a smile or even a look that acknowledged that he still thought of Sam. Now, twenty years later, he was still marked by the young man, his shameful secret locked up inside, he found that his cocksucker desires had never left and were never satisfied again and it tormented him.

Sam's wife was shaking him, "Hey, honey, it's almost 6:30 already," and he felt her hand on his shoulder again.

He sprang to life, "Shit, how did I oversleep today?" He took the coffee that she handed to him and swallowed quickly. "Thanks honey, you're the best," and he kissed her cheek before heading for the shower.

Today he needed to look his best, but by 7 am, he had run

out of time and it was all details at this point. Showered, hair slicked back, his tie worked with the suit and he checked his cuffs and secured the tie bar. He was making the presentation of his life this morning, meeting his new boss and standing at the front of the board room, discussing the sales figures that had taken weeks to perfect, he was confident but nervous. He would have been calmer if he'd been able to wake up slowly and progress through his normal morning routine, but he told himself, as he drew his shoulders back, walking through the steel and glass foyer of his office building, he knew it well, probably far better than the new boss.

When he entered the room, bustling with co-workers, Sam got several slaps on the back and smiles and handshakes, he was good at his job as well as meticulous in general; everyone had faith in him. The clock pointed at 10 am sharp and he stood at attention, behind the podium, waiting for the new manager to arrive.

The double doors at the back of the room clicked and slid open and a tall man with inky black hair and caramel-colored skin walked in the room. He was powerfully built; it was obvious even under the pin-striped suit that his broad shoulders and muscular arms could barely be contained. He had an air of confidence and walked like an animal that was hunting. He caught Sam's eye and the smile showed a gleaming line of pearly whites and his dark eyes locked Sam in his gaze.

For a moment, he was back on twin bed, hunkered over the sticky cock that he couldn't get enough of, he could almost hear the wet noises that came from his mouth as he took greedy, sucking gulps.

Sam shook his head quickly to ban the thought, get it out of his head, this was not the time or the place and this was his new boss, the man in charge of his career. He smiled back and strode to greet him, hand out. "Hi, I'm Sam, you must be Mr. Richards."

The large man's hand easily covered his own much smaller, white one and Sam knew that he could have crushed his hand if had chosen to, rather than shake it. "That's right, nice to meet you," he commanded direct eye contact and when Sam dared to delve into the dark pools, he found heat that hit him with a wave of desire that almost overwhelmed him.

Hands still locked together, Sam was suddenly hot and aware that every eye in the room was on him. There was no time to melt back into the past where at some point he had served a Master gratefully and humbly on his knees. Sam hoped that no one else could hear his heart pounding and assumed his position at the podium.

Once the presentation was over, the applause was furious and handshakes and slaps on the back were all around. Sam smiled and heard the buzz of the conversation around him, nodded his head when it seemed that he needed to agree but his thoughts were elsewhere. At the back of the room sat Mr. Richards, his thick thighs were spread in the seat and Sam could see the quads poking at an angle in his pants and the desire to kneel there and place his hands on the man's muscular legs while he waited to be guided was almost overwhelming. His only chance to save himself from the humiliation was to leave.

Back at his desk, Sam berated himself for his behavior. This man was his boss, he held his career in his hands, but when he thought of the powerful hands on his he immediately melted into the daydream of the hands on his neck while he pushed Sam's mouth down to serve.

The phone call came minutes before Sam was leaving and as soon as he heard the voice; his face was hot and flushed once more.

"Sam? It's Gabriel Richards, do you have a moment?" his voice was as commanding as his presence.

"Yes, sir," Sam sat gingerly on the edge of his seat, with sweaty palms and a cock that strained to be released, he waited for directions.

"I need you to come up to my office," the word need made

Sam gulp for air.

"Yes, sir," he added hopefully, "right now?"

"Yes, as soon as you can," his boss hung up and Sam replaced the receiver in the cradle and felt the flush and the tingle run the course of his body as he grabbed his jacket and briefcase and made his way to the elevator.

Outside of Mr. Richards' office, he paused, trying to collect himself. It was highly possible that the man only wanted to discuss the presentation, or even question his numbers, this could all be work related. The crush was more likely his alone. Sam had experienced this a few times over the years since his servitude had come to an end. He was married, attracted to women, stared at his wife's bountiful curves and masturbated regularly to girls in magazines as well as the sexy blond who lived down the block. She jogged with her dogs every morning, tight yoga pants skimming her perfect thighs and her large breasts clamped down in the pink jogging bra, a sheen of sweat on her cheeks.

He was a straight man and never thought of himself as anything else, and for most of the last twenty years, he could dismiss the semester of sucking his Master's cock as a phase. Then out of nowhere, a dark-skinned, muscular man would cross his path and Sam would feel the undeniable longing run down the length of his body and his mouth would water, sometimes he'd have to wipe the puddle of drool off his chin. The man would become his obsession and all of his fantasies spun out of control, the blond neighbor was a faint blip on the radar and his dick merely pulsed when she ran by him. He gave in to his cocksucker desires and it was maddening.

None of his other crushes had ever acknowledged him and Sam had never had the courage to volunteer. It had been twenty years since the boy in his dorm room had violated him and since then, the hunger pains had seemed to grow. As he entered his boss' large office and walked toward the man sitting behind the massive desk, he realized that the wave of want that washed over him was just beyond the limits of his self-control.

"Sam, sit down," the man gestured to a long, low black leather sofa to the right and Sam did as commanded, watching Mr. Richards walk across the floor to join him. He sat as he had in the chair earlier, large, powerful thighs parted, shoulders up so that his long arms reached across almost the entire length of the couch. Sam noticed that one hand reached behind his shoulder, they were almost touching. His skin felt hot there.

"Great presentation today, you did an outstanding job," Gabriel met his eye again and Sam's erection responded.

"Thank you, sir," he mumbled, trying to draw himself up and put his shoulders back where they should be and talk man to man.

"I wanted to speak to you in private though about something," Mr. Richards turned on the couch so that his enormous bulge in his pants was front and center in Sam's line of vision. A whimper was there in his throat, if he spoke, it would come out so Sam clamped his lips shut.

"I noticed today, and you're doing it again right now," Gabriel's voice was lower and more intimate and seemed to inch down his spine, touching him all along his body. "You really can't help yourself, can you? You need to suck my cock."

The words were finally out there, tangible, he couldn't deny it if he had wanted to. Sam couldn't find his voice either and simply shook his head up and down in agreement.

"You look like a cocksucker, Sam, in fact, you look like you would like to devour this big, black cock," and Mr. Richards' hand moved to the crotch of his pants and Sam's eyes followed down as the moved the weight of his dick to a more comfortable position. "Isn't that right, Sam?"

The voice that answered was squeaky and higher than he had ever remembered speaking before. "Yes sir."

"Yes sir what?" Gabriel was going to force him to say the words that he'd been swallowing down since the first day on the bed.

"Yes, sir, I want to suck your cock. I want to be your slave," he was trembling all over his body and he moved his hands to loosen his tie which suddenly seemed to choke him.

"Oh, my slave?" Mr. Richards took his jacket off, never taking his eyes away from Sam. "Have you served another Master, Sam?"

"Only once before, sir," and the longing that had been left behind, unanswered all this time, was clear in his tone.

"But you've obviously wanted to serve ever since, in fact I don't know if I ever remember seeing a man who wanted to suck my dick more," he was unbuttoning his shirt now, Sam could see the dark line of hair that ran from between his erect nipples, down the rippled muscles on his stomach, down into the pants that still hid the man's thick dick. "I am a very disciplined Master though Sam, there are rules when a little, white cocksucker serves me."

"Yes, sir?" Sam's erection pulsated and his precum wet his underwear and the spot was growing on the crotch of his pants.

"First of all, my slaves know that they have to earn the right to wear clothes when in my presence. When you present yourself, slave Sam, you will be naked and on your knees," suddenly Sam wondered why he hadn't done that in the first place. He stood up and with shaking hands slipped off the tie, unbuttoned the shirt, pushed down his pants and in a moment, stood naked before his boss.

"Look at your pathetic, tiny cock," Gabriel was smirking at him, his erection drooled and beckoned at the man, slapping Sam's thigh and quivering at the attention it received. "You are almost a woman, you know that cocksucker?"

"Yes, sir," Sam melted, his knees buckling, and he found himself in the supplicant position that he knew was appropriate.

"Do you fuck your wife with that tiny, little thing?" the huge man wanted to know and the amused look on his face suggested that he was imagining how it was even possible.

"Yes, sir," Sam knew it happened but could think about nothing but performing his slave duties.

"Once you prove yourself to be a good slave, perhaps I'll have to fuck her as well," his smile and his pearly white teeth gleamed and he licked his lips. "You'll love watching your wife become a slave for black cock too. You'll both get on your knees for it, won't you?"

Sam pictured his wife, mouth open, tongue out, lapping up thick rivulets of the man's steamy cum and he could hear her moan, the idea made his dick lurch and he squeaked out, "Yes, sir."

Gabriel unbuckled his belt and ran his zipper down to the bottom, he pushed his pants down past his angled hips and his monstrous dick was out. Sam couldn't breathe when he looked at it, long, wide, the dark skin shone and he chuckled when Sam let out a long sigh.

"You want that in your mouth now, don't you?" the big man murmured.

"Yes, sir, please let me serve you," Sam was inching forward on his knees so that he could wait between the man's legs, close enough to smell his sex and see the clear liquid that bubbled up from his slit.

"Get on the couch, with your ass in the air, slave," Gabriel patted the leather beside him.

Sam was in position, his mouth only inches from the largest cock he'd ever seen.

"Your ass will be mine as well, slave," Gabriel could easily reach his bottom from where he sat; his right hand slapped his bare cheeks. "Did you give your ass to your Master, white boy?"

The wide, hot palm on his cool, pale skin seemed to burn. He felt his stomach churn but his hard-on quivered at the idea. "No, sir."

"Then you have not been a true slave, Sam," his boss explained, "to be a true cock slave and give yourself to a Master means that your mouth and your ass are to be used, at any time your Master wishes," Sam was mesmerized as Gabriel brought his thick index finger up to his mouth, wet it and then slowly brought it back to between his upturned cheeks. "The only way a slave can cum is when he is giving pleasure to his Master, and only with permission, do you understand, Sam?"

Sam felt the finger stroking his tender, puckered skin around his asshole and he couldn't explain why he tilted his hips up to give the man access to his hole. He had never before thought of a man entering him and now, it seemed to be a dangerous combination of shameful and too hot for words. He heard himself moan as Gabriel's wet finger swirled around the sensitive skin there.

"That's right, slave, while you suck your Master's big, black cock, you'll know that I'm inside your other hole as well," and the tip of his index finger pushed inside, an inch and then another, the sensation of being filled there sent a current of desire racing down his body. "A good cock slave will be full of his Master's cum and his piss. Are you ready to become my slave then, Sam?"

His cheeks were hot and the sweat ran down his neck and his heart throbbed in his throat and everything screamed at him to say no, but the truth tumbled out of his open mouth along with a groan that he had been holding back for too long. "Yes, Master," he panted and pushed his bottom back on the finger to give him access to his virginity.

"Then suck my cock, little slave," Gabriel took his invitation and skewered him, his long, thick finger all the way inside him now, to the base, and Sam bent his head and opened his mouth as wide as he could to get the beautiful dick as deep inside as possible.

The bulging head was soaked in precum and Sam slathered his tongue across the width of it to drink the salty liquid down, loving the taste of his Master, the tip of his tongue lapped at his large slit and he felt the beads that emerged on his tongue, swallowing them in careful gulps. He reached forward to grasp the solid base of his Master's cock with his small hand and his Master pulled him up by the hair.

"Not your hands, slave, only your mouth," and Sam quickly withdrew his hand and pushed his head forward, his lips spread wide and his tongue dancing along the pronounced ridge under the bulbous head. Deeper, he moved forward feeling his Master's head touch the roof of his mouth and spill his brine there while his lips wrapped tightly around the shaft. Only half of the enormous dick was inside him and he worked his way down so that the huge head hovered at the opening of his throat.

"Swallow my cock, slave, worship the big, black dick that owns you now," his Master knew exactly what he longed to do and Sam moaned on his solid flesh as he pumped back and forth to take more and more of the meaty erection inside his wet mouth.

Gabriel's finger stirred now, buried in his asshole, it had opened him and then waited; now he beckoned with the finger, touching a place deep inside that made Sam's tiny penis dribble and shudder with delight. Sam's mouth stretched open wide and he sucked his Master to the base of his perfect cock, soaking him with his saliva, drawing his head back and plunging it forward, he ran his tongue along every inch and lapped up the sweet juices that ran down the length of him now.

"This is your place, cocksucker," Gabriel now thrust his cock up and down, deep inside, the dick was in Sam's throat and he relaxed to take it in as far as it would go, impaled and deep throating him now, he whimpered like a whore. "With your mouth and your slut hole full of a real man. As a slave to big, black cock, your only purpose is to give yourself to your alpha Master whenever you are told."

Gabriel was fucking his face now and his asshole, spreading both open wide and the pleasure that weaved its way up, his prostate throbbing with the delight of his Master's touch was bringing him to the brink of his own shivering orgasm. Gabriel seemed to know exactly what was happening in his white slave's body, and murmured now, "A white man should only cum when his black Master is using him for his pleasure," and his thrusts came faster, his finger moved relentlessly, rocking the soft ridge in Sam's ass that sent him to the edge, the huge dick filling every inch of his wet mouth.

Gabriel grabbed him by the hair and force fed him the cock now, holding him down, he was desperate to taste the wads of hot, buttery cum that would erupt from his Master's black dick and the first huge spurt entered his throat and ran down, deep inside. Sam moved his head up and drank the next just as hungrily. Once Gabriel's grip relaxed, he was able to wrap his lips around the head that shuddered in his mouth, spitting ropes of his salty cream, his Master's release went on and on and Sam drank every drop.

The finger that had opened his virgin hole still moved inside and Sam was trembling with his Master's touch. Still lapping his tongue along the solid head of the man's dick, cleaning every drop of his sweet cum, Gabriel asked, "Do you wish to cum now, with my finger inside you?"

Sam hadn't imagined that he'd be allowed and looked up to his Master gratefully and pleaded, "Yes, please, Master."

"That's right, tell me slave, tell me who you belong to," his Master wasn't going to stop until he confessed it all.

"I belong to you Master," he was tightening his anus around the finger and moving to meet the movements inside him, getting fucked for the first time, he realized that he loved the sensation of his Master in all of his holes. "I will suck your cock whenever you let me and I will give you my ass to do whatever you please with it. I will gladly drink your cum and piss whenever you give it to me because that is what a white cock slave longs to do for his big, black alpha Master."

He started bucking and clenching the finger and his words were forcing the orgasm out of him as he realized that it was all true and it was all he had wanted.

"Then you may cum, slave," his Master granted it and almost spontaneously, Sam erupted, his small dick jolting in his hand, he came and jerked and shivered until the puddle of his own want coated his hand.

When Gabriel removed the finger, he immediately longed to be filled again, his ass felt empty and he ached to be stretched open wide, to take his Master's cock inside, on his knees, on the couch, bent over and filled to the bottom with the bulging dick. "Taste yourself, slave," Gabriel wanted him to lick off the finger that had been buried inside him and without hesitating, Sam opened his mouth and sucked up the juice from his virgin hole. "And your cum," Gabriel pointed to his hand that was still grasping his withered, small penis. Sam brought his hand to his mouth and licked up the puddle as well.

"Very good, cocksucker," Gabriel looked pleased and Sam basked in the knowledge that he had served well. "Now, after I mark you, you will be my slave and mine alone. Is that understood?"

"Yes, Master," Sam wanted nothing else.

"You will do my bidding and make yourself available to me at any time I command, is that clear?" the big man was standing now, and Sam knew that his place was once again on his knees.

"Yes, Master," he looked up; his Master's dick was softer than it had been, still thick and the dark flesh shone with cum and his wet mouth.

"Open your mouth slave," he prompted and Sam did, feeling the warm trickle of piss run down his throat. He swallowed and drank; closing his mouth for one moment and his Master's hot essence spilled on his lips and trickled down his chin and neck, dribbling to his chest. When his Master was done pissing, he could feel it in his stomach, he was absolutely full of the man and a thought ran across his mind, what would it be like to feel his Master's seed seeping from his ass? He knew that he would obsess over the image until it happened.

Once more, his Master knew him too well and said, "Tomorrow night, I will take your virginity. Then you'll be properly filled in both of your slave holes," and then, as if he knew he must remind him, "You are not allowed to cum until then, slave, remember that. You'll only cum on your Master's dick."

"Yes, Master," Sam almost sobbed with want. The man knew everything, every inky, twisted fantasy that he'd been replaying over and over in his mind all this time.

"You're going to do just fine then slave," Gabriel had started to dress, he was sending Sam away, satisfied, yet wanting so much more. "Now that you know what you are and what you were meant to be."

Sam looked up and his voice was soft, trembling a bit as he called it out, "I am a natural cocksucker."

"Very good, slave, very good."

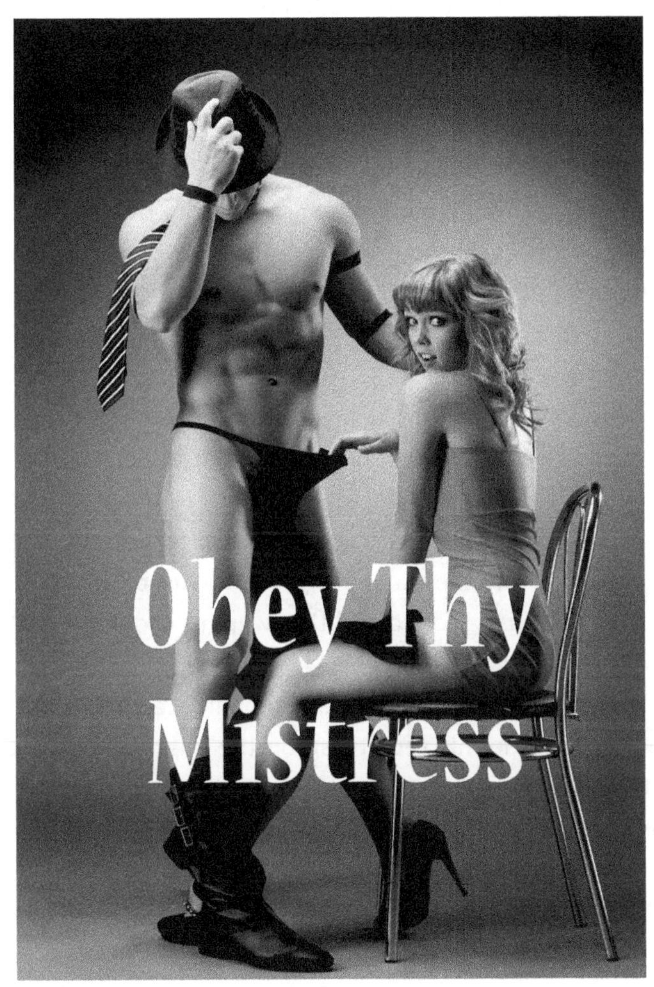
Obey Thy
Mistress

The afternoon was dragging by so slowly, David couldn't help watching the clock but minutes passed like hours and by the time 4:00 came, he was twitching and his pulse was racing. It was almost here and it had seemed like an eternity since last weekend. During the week, he would come home to Amelia and grab a beer, watch her cook dinner, sometimes even grab her waist from behind while rubbing himself on her bouncing bottom. If anything, their weekends had made him want her more; he could hardly keep his hands off of her. On Friday at 5 pm though, everything changed.

Finally, it was time and he grabbed the overnight bag that had been sitting on the floor by his desk all day, tempting him with its contents, and said good-bye to his co-workers. Peter, the man who sat in the cubicle next to him asked, "So what's on for the weekend, David?"

He could hardly hold on to the handles of the bag, his palms were sweaty, the overwhelming sensation of nerves and excitement would build all week to a crescendo and on Friday afternoons, it was all he could do not to explode. He licked his lips before replying, "Oh, the usual, hanging out with the wife."

His colleague scoffed and threw up his shoulders, "Well, try to have fun with that."

David couldn't get away fast enough. He almost ran to the car and once inside, his secret bag on the passenger seat next to him, it was all he could do to drive to the agreed spot, hands trembling, heart pounding, every Friday afternoon was the same. He pulled into the hotel parking lot and made his way past the lobby, glancing over to the left at the blond girl at the front desk, trying not to stare.

In the men's room, he locked the door behind him and the weekend began.

He stared at himself in the mirror and loosened the tie that had been choking him all day, unbuttoning his shirt and kicking off the loafers, he already felt more relaxed. Once his dress pants were off and the boxers that he had been leaking into all day were folded and shoved in the bag, he was free. David gently pulled up the pink, satin panties that he had brought especially for this weekend and exhaled in relief. Daisy could come out and play.

Daisy shaved her body daily, keeping her skin silky smooth for her Mistress was a high priority, and Mistress Amelia was stringent about girls taking care of their bodies. She rubbed the pink lotion on her legs and arms again; soft, little girls got cuddled much more often.

The breasts that Daisy used in her bra were a sad reminder that she had none of her own, but once the pink bra was hooked into place, her curves were worth it and she reminded herself of Mistress' promise, perhaps if she were a good girl and served well, one day the prosthetic breasts would be real and hers. She touched herself gently over the bra and could see the gel-like nipples protruding through the fabric. She could only imagine right now what it would feel like to have a mouth gently sucking on them, but just the picture of it, a tall, handsome man with his lips wrapped tight around her hard, pink bud, Daisy's head thrown back in ecstasy and her clitty shuddering from the sensation, it was almost too much for her.

No point in letting herself get carried away right now, there was much more work to be done and Mistress Amelia would punish her for being tardy. She slid the white slip over her head and buttoned herself into the dress, black with white polka dots, a fitted waist and a short, full skirt that showed her long, lean legs. Once the white thigh high stockings were pulled up, Daisy was careful to make sure that the seams were straight in the back as Mistress had taught her, she strapped on the hot, pink heels. They were the one slutty indulgence that Mistress had allowed and one glance in the full-length mirror on the wall made her gasp. The price that she had paid for being allowed to wear those was entirely worth it.

She swirled the foundation on with both index fingers, the way Mistress had shown her, tapping the blush brush gently she gave herself rosy cheeks. Mistress Amelia said it should look like she was flushed from an orgasm, not like a whore, Mistress had been so kind to transform her from a common tart to a lady. Well, Daisy wasn't sure if all of her behavior could be described as ladylike and when she remembered what Mistress forced her to do for the shoes, she actually needed no rouge.

A little eye shadow made her blue eyes pop and the false eyelashes that she fluttered instinctively whenever an Alpha male looked her way almost completed her, the only thing missing was the pink, shimmering gloss that Mistress liked to see on her full, pouty lips. When Daisy was done applying it, she puckered and kissed the air, as she'd seen Marilyn Monroe do in pictures. She wondered if it were true, did gentlemen prefer blondes? She was about to find out.

The wig was almost platinum, long curls down the back and she carefully fitted it over her short, brown hair. Daisy brushed it carefully the way she had been taught, shaking out the curls that touched the tender skin on the back of her neck, the hot blond in the mirror was about to take a stroll. Everything was back in her bag and Daisy unlocked the bathroom door.

A man pushed it open immediately and she screeched, she wasn't ready for someone to just barge in and her heart was in her throat when the dark-haired man walked in. He looked at her quizzically at first, then a slow smile spread across his handsome, dimpled face, "aren't you in the wrong place, Miss?" he asked in a deep voice.

Daisy cleared her throat, her high-pitched voice cracked sometimes when she was nervous, "I guess so, I got confused," she giggled and shrugged her shoulders.

"Well, you should come in the men's room more often," he spoke to her, walking backwards slowly to the urinals, obviously attracted, he didn't want to turn away. "You're very pretty," he seemed embarrassed suddenly and turned to face the wall, his hand reaching the front of his pants, Daisy heard him unzip.

Her hand was on the handle but she couldn't make herself

leave. This was not allowed, but she was so hungry, so needy and the sight of herself in the mirror was so alluring, she heard her heels click across the tile as she walked toward him.

"Whoa!" he glanced over his shoulder at Daisy, still pissing; he looked a little worried as she continued to advance. She looked over his shoulder, his thick cock was in his hand and the stream flowed from his large slit and Daisy's limp, pink clitty dribbled in the satin panties as she watched. "Didn't expect you to watch me piss," his expression was both uncomfortable and turned on. "See something you like?"

"Oh yes," she sounded breathy now, just like a horny, blond bimbo would, she clasped her hands together behind her back to stop herself from reaching out to grab what she wanted.

He shook the last droplets off and turned to her, no longer uncomfortable, his expression was sheer lust, and he asked, "Would you like to taste it then?"

Daisy slid to her knees, she knew that her white stockings would show the dirt and Mistress would know exactly what she had been up to, but it was a worry that flitted in the back of her mind, the cock controlled her and forced her to do its bidding. She opened her pink, slick lips and showed the man her eager tongue.

"Jesus Christ, you really do want to suck my cock, don't you?" the tall, broad man didn't wait for an answer and fed the moist head to her with a moan, Daisy knew that he was looking down at her, watching her tongue lap along his slit and although she secretly wished that she had drank down a mouthful of his piss first, the taste of what was left behind was almost enough.

"Baby," she murmured, looking up from the floor and fluttering her eyelashes, "I need to suck your cock, I want it all down in my throat," and to prove it, Daisy forced her mouth down on him, filling herself with the thick dick and the hard, round head touched the top of her throat as she found her pink lips wrapped around the bottom of his shaft.

"God, oh you're mouth feels so good, it's so wet," the man

above her was thrusting in and out and his dick tasted so good, his manly, earthy scent was in Daisy's nostrils and she reached up to fondle his heavy, taut ball sack, feeling the weight of the hot load that he would deposit in her throat.

Daisy wanted to make it last and she slid up to the head again and watched him as she teased him gently along the ridge under his head and then slathered his shaft with her tongue, all the way up and all the way down, her hand tightened its grip at the meaty base and she continued to wet his skin with her mouth.

"Fuck, you are a dirty girl, aren't you?" he was groaning as he continued to pump, wanting to drive it all the back inside her in one fast, hard push.

"I'm a filthy, nasty slut and I live to suck a real man's cock," even just saying the words herself sent a shiver all the way down Daisy's prone body and she immediately did as he wanted and force fed herself the man's engorged penis. She felt him tense, his balls were tight and she could hardly wait to taste every salty drop of his orgasm. She sucked harder and faster, her nose buried in his dark pubic hair, she kept the head of his dick at the opening of her throat and stretched her mouth wide to swallow it all.

"You are a nasty slut, I'm gonna cum so hard," it was all he had time to say and Daisy wrapped her hands around his solid thighs to feel them shake as he unleashed the first hot spurt in her esophagus. The cream ran down her throat and she pulled back an inch to taste the next hard dash on her tongue, swallowing quickly; she pursed her pink lips around the head to suck the rest out right from the source.

The man was panting and grinding his hips against her face as she took his hot load and when the last dribble was licked up; Daisy saw him rest his head against the wall and heard his contented sigh. "What a great way to start the weekend!" he stood up straight to zip his fly and suddenly, looked uncomfortable once more and prepared for a quick exit, "thank you!" he said before walking swiftly out of the bathroom.

He never heard Daisy whimper, "No, thank you."

"You're late, sissy," Mistress Amelia snarled at her as soon as she heard the door close behind her. Try as she might to clean up, Daisy knew that as soon as her Mistress saw her, she would guess the rest. She walked resolutely to the living room and curtseyed, keeping her eyes on the floor, she trembled as she imagined what the punishment might be, but she knew she deserved it.

"Oh, look at the sissy faggot," Mistress clicked her tongue and spoke to her with sheer disdain, "couldn't even keep your tramp hole shut until this evening. Were you sucking a dick this afternoon, Daisy?" her voice was like ice in Daisy's veins and she knew that lying was inadvisable.

"Yes, ma'am, I'm sorry," her chin shook and her high, little voice squeaked as she confessed.

The doorbell rang and Mistress Amelia looked up coolly, "go get the door Daisy and we'll speak about this later," her eyebrow was up on her forehead and for a moment, Daisy forgot herself, drawn to Mistress' beautiful face, her jet, black hair was up in a bun, her dark eyes shone and her red lips looked ripe and ready to be kissed. "Go now!" her voice snapped Daisy back to reality and she scurried to get the door.

There were two men on the stoop, the tan one at the front leaned on the door in a familiar way, as if he had been here often and was used to letting himself in. The white man in the back was shorter, wider and offered a friendly smile to Daisy when she poked her head out, "Can I help you?" she asked the gentlemen.

"Get out of the way, sissy freak," the tan one replied, barging past Daisy, heading for the living room, "we're here to see your wife," and the two men made their way through the kitchen quickly to get to Mistress Amelia.

Daisy heard her sounds of delight as she welcomed them and imagined that her kissable lips were already being embraced by her two lovers. "Bring some drinks, slut," Mistress called to Daisy and she started to prepare the tray. She carried it slowly to the living room, walking in the slut shoes with shaking hands; she tried desperately not to spill.

Mistress Amelia was on the couch, her head in the caramel-skinned lover's lap and her dainty bare feet with the red toenails were caressing the other man's obvious erection through his pants. "Set it down, slut," she directed Daisy as the tan lover reached out to fondle her breast under the opening at the front of her dress.

"In your sissy position, cock whore," she instructed Daisy and watched with a smirk as the girl's legs shook until she made her way to the carpet, "look at how well she gets on her knees," she commented to her two lovers and Daisy's cheeks burned when she heard their laughter.

"The little bimbo couldn't wait until she got home to get a mouthful of cum, the little faggot had to suck someone off in the bathroom," Mistress Amelia would enjoy telling all of the nasty details to her Alphas, "So what should the slut's punishment be?"

The three of them conspired in whispers and stolen kisses, Mistress Amelia would glance over to Daisy occasionally and laugh her head back, the broad, white man kissed her throat and Daisy swallowed hard to keep down the panic. "That's perfect!" Mistress Amelia exclaimed and pointed one long, red nail in Daisy's direction.

"Go get the five gallon bucket from under the sink, cunt," she commanded and Daisy fetched it and returned quickly, her knees knocking as she stood and waited for the next direction. "The boys have decided that since you like it in the bathroom so much, that you should only drink piss this weekend, how do you like that, Miss Daisy?"

Daisy's answer was unimportant and the shame pulsated through her as well as the excitement, like all of Mistress Amelia's punishments, it was exquisite.

"On your knees then faggot, so you can wash some of that cum down," and Daisy scrambled to get into position, kneeling in front of the bucket that the tan man stood in front of, he unzipped to reveal his massive, dark, uncircumcised penis and held it tight at the root, shaking it with his hand, just inches from Daisy's face.

"You like that, don't you whore?" his voice was as powerful as his frame and Daisy's body shook in response to him.

"Yes, it's beautiful," her little girl voice was quiet, she was in awe of his size and inhaled his scent and waited until she was told what to do.

"Open your mouth, then slut, stick out your tongue and show me what a sissy does when she sees a real dick," Mistress Amelia was watching Daisy's every move from the couch as her paler lover unbuttoned the front of her dress and stroked her lovely breasts under the bra.

Daisy readied herself, opened her mouth, showed the lover her eager tongue and closed her eyes quickly and shrieked when a burst of hot piss ran down her throat and then splattered across her face. She could hear the urine running from her face to the bucket underneath her and felt the lover continue once more, hot, sticky liquid coated her closed lips until she opened them and started to drink. "That's right, slut, drink it up, let it wash all that cum down," Mistress Amelia chuckled wickedly as she watched her lover squirt Daisy down the front of her dress, she was soaked in the Alpha's urine now, marked by the man like property. Daisy's clitty squirmed at the thought.

"Baby," Mistress Amelia murmured to her lover when the brown lover was finished and returned to her on the couch, his cock still out, the enormous dick fluttered as he approached her and her hand reached out to pull him close. Her other lover left the couch to approach Daisy and this time, she steadied herself, ready to perform her duty.

The stocky man smirked as he unzipped, his cock was even meatier than the first man's, shorter, pink, but the girth was incredible and Daisy whimpered as she pictured herself trying to stretch her mouth open wide enough to encompass her lips around him. "You'd love to suck that dick, wouldn't you whore?" the man looked down at her and stroked her face tenderly.

Daisy shook her head yes and parted her lips to invite him inside.

The lover slapped her face with his solid shaft, once, twice on the one side and a third time on the other cheek and mocked her, "that's for your wife, faggot, all you get is piss," and the warm trickle of his liquid started. He pressed the head of his cock against Daisy's upper lip, knowing she wasn't allowed to suck him, it was torture to feel it so near and yet so far away and all she could do was open her mouth and drink.

Daisy heard her soft, girlish moans, her mouth open, her wet, swallowing noises as she took his stream down her throat. His piss gushed out of the sides of her mouth and spilled into the bucket below and once he was finished, she watched him shake his cock and felt the last few drops spit across her cheeks. When she looked down to the bucket below, she heard her heart beat fast in her eardrums when she imagined what Mistress Amelia would command her to do next.

"What are you waiting for, whore?" her Mistress asked, Daisy looked up to see that her dress was off and she wore only the tiny, black bra and thong and the dark lover's dick was in her hand as the other man pressed his lips to the sliver of fabric between her legs. "Drink it, bitch," Mistress curled her lip as she stared at Daisy.

Daisy's hands shook and she closed her eyes, bent her head, raised the piss bucket up to her mouth and drank the contents down. She swallowed it quickly, not sure if she could hold it all inside, determined not to let it come up and have to repeat the process, she clamped her hand over her lips when she set the bucket down.

"Very good, sissy," Mistress Amelia noted, "however, I just realized that you are overdressed for the rest of tonight's duties. Go upstairs, take your dress off and wait for me in the bathroom."

Daisy reluctantly trudged upstairs, she hated to be ignored

and didn't want to miss one moment of Mistress Amelia with her lovers, but she knew that disobedience would result in swift and painful justice, so she followed her instructions and slipped the dress and slip off over her head, readjusted her hair and knelt on the cold tile in wait.

Daisy closed her eyes and remembered sucking the gorgeous man's cock on her knees earlier and moaned as she recalled vividly every thick inch pushing into her mouth and she felt her tiny nub rise and dribble in her pink panties. Mistress Amelia still hadn't come up and with no one to direct her, Daisy held her cockette tightly in her hand, over the panties, grinding the damp, satiny material against her hard stump.

The door opened with a bang and Daisy immediately let her clitty go, hanging her head as Mistress Amelia approached her, tugging her chin up to look her in the eye. "Were you just touching yourself, cum bucket?" she asked Daisy in a low voice.

It would be easy for Mistress Amelia to see and lying would only push her further, so Daisy nodded and whispered, "Yes ma'am."

"You know," her Mistress continued, "I may not let you cum at all this weekend if you can't control yourself, do you understand?"

The thought of being denied after faithful servitude terrified Daisy and she quickly agreed, "I'll be good, I'm sorry Mistress."

"Get in the tub, faggot," was her only reply.

Daisy felt her legs shake as she made her way, stepping daintily into the tub and descending to her prone position, head to the bottom, and ass in the air. "You never douched your slut hole today, did you cunt?" Mistress Amelia already knew the answer.

"No, ma'am," Daisy replied.

"Lucky for you, I have just the solution," her Mistress sounded amused and it made Daisy nervous. "Come on in, gentlemen," Daisy couldn't see the lovers enter the bathroom but knew that they were there, "my little piss bitch needs some more, I think," and Daisy knew she was kissing one and felt the other man behind her in the tub.

"Just yank down those panties," Mistress Amelia told the man, "she doesn't deserve to wear them if she can't act like a lady," and Daisy felt the strong hands run down the back of her dirty stockings as the man slid her wet panties down and exposed her pussy.

"Oh yeah, I'm gonna fill you up, you nasty little cunt," Daisy recognized the darker lover's voice and felt him behind her now, he must be naked, the hair on his thighs bristled against her and sent a quiver all the way down her legs. Without another word and without any lube, Daisy felt the man force his way inside and impale her tight, little hole with his huge cock. The combination of pain and pleasure coursed through her trembling body as she moaned from both and arched her back for more.

"He's not fucking you, slut," Mistress Amelia laughed heartlessly as she watched Daisy ask for more, "tonight your douche is piss, you get to hold it inside and feel it inside your pussy, sloshing around, working its way up deeper and deeper," her voice was mesmerizing and Daisy tightened her pussy around the pole inside her when she felt the first warm spurt inside, "you like it in the bathroom so much, you can stay here, faggot."

The man inside her was filling her with piss, she could feel the stream flowing up, just as Mistress Amelia said it would, deeper and deeper, her pussy was stretched and flooded with liquid, the cock opening her and the wide head pressed against her g-spot, but with no friction, it was all just a torturous tease. Daisy couldn't help but beg, "Please, sir, please fuck me."

Mistress Amelia barked at him, "I told you, slut, no one is fucking you tonight! You had your dick for the day," and the first lover pushed the last trickle inside and withdrew, leaving Daisy gasping and full, horny and aching, her sad little clitty drooled up her belly and it dripped on her thigh. "I'm going to plug you up now, slut," Mistress Amelia shoved something solid inside Daisy, her thick, pink butt plug, she imagined, and told her, "and just to keep your hands off yourself," Mistress grabbed her by the wrists and tied a knot around each, attaching the other end of the rope to the faucet.

"Nighty night, bimbo," Mistress Amelia said in a mocking tone before turning out the light and leaving Daisy alone in the tub.

In a few minutes, she could hear her Mistress and her lovers in the bedroom and imagined in detail what was happening. She heard her Mistress calling out, "God, yes fuck me with that big cock," and Daisy realized that her true punishment was that she would be forced to listen and imagine, but didn't get to watch. For the first time since that afternoon, she regretted what a cock whore she was.

Mistress Amelia came again and again with the two men and Daisy pictured every move, she could see in her mind's eye her Mistress' red lips wrapped around one man's thick cock and the other man behind her, pumping in and out rapidly, his dick coated in her sweet juices. When she heard a man moaning and shouting, she imagined that the lover had climaxed deep inside her Mistress and she licked her lips, seeing her delectable crevice dripping with his torrents of hot cream. Why had she been so stupid? She should be there to lick up every last drop.

Daisy lost track of time, it could have been hours that she knelt, bottom up, the Alpha's piss still plugged up inside her, churning back and forth in her aching cunt, listening to her Mistress take her pleasure again and again. She jumped when the bathroom light came back on.

"Have you learned your lesson, little girl?" Mistress Amelia's long, red nail scraped down her back.

"Yes, ma'am," Daisy shook her head yes, the cold porcelain rubbing her forehead, "I'm sorry, I won't suck anymore cock without your permission," she didn't know if it were true or not but she heard the sorrow in her voice and hoped that Mistress Amelia would set her free.

"Well, even though I'm sure that's a lie, I believe you've been punished enough for one night," Mistress knew that Daisy was an incorrigible little whore but she untied the rope anyway and added, "I'm pulling out your plug, slut, hold on."

She withdrew the plug and Daisy felt the gush of urine spill down her thighs and she sighed, she was exactly where she deserved to be. "Now, get yourself cleaned up slut," Mistress Amelia instructed and left Daisy to daydream in the shower. It was only Friday; she could only imagine what her Mistress had in store for her the rest of the weekend.

Monday had flown by; David had been busy making phone calls for most of it and was surprised to see that it was almost 4:00 already. In an hour or two, he'd go home to Amelia; he smiled to himself when he pictured his wife's face. The love of his life, he was just damn lucky that she was so good to him.

He made his way down the hall to the men's room and walked to the urinal, unzipping and fishing out his dick, he whistled a little tune as he went to the bathroom. He never heard the door open but he heard it lock. David turned his head, startled, and as he slowly recognized the man standing there, his face was hot and his stomach churned. What had Daisy done now?

"Hey, you look different than the last time I saw you in a bathroom," the man whose face and dick David remembered in perfect detail said as he took three quick steps and reached him at the urinal, "but that doesn't mean you can't suck my cock just as good," with one hand, the man was pushing David down by the shoulder and with the other he was bringing out the big dick that had started it all.

David was weak regardless of what he wore and the man's hand easily maneuvered him to the floor, he looked up with apprehension, his lips open but he clamped his mouth closed as recalled the events and Mistress Amelia's vicious punishment. David shook his head no and whispered, "I can't."

"Come on, sissy," the man held his engorged, beautiful dick in hand, the head was dribbling with his precum and David flashed to watch Daisy choke on it and he could almost taste the salty essence on his tongue. There had been an absence of cock for the weekend and his hunger had built, not allowed a release, his slut holes were both hungry and for a moment he wanted to slide his pants down and beg the man to fuck both of them. His wet clitty stirred in his boxers and he almost let out a long sigh when he stopped.

"Wait, what do you mean, sissy?" he asked, David's heart was beating so loudly he thought the man must be able to hear it. How did he know?

"Your wife told me where to find you, cunt," the man laughed as he pressed the fleshy head of his bulging dick to David's bottom lip, "suck it up, little girl."

David felt the shiver run down his spine as he relinquished control and did exactly what he said he wouldn't do, knowing that the punishment would be exquisite, he heard himself beg in the small, girlish voice, "yes, please give it to me," before opening his mouth wide.

More Books by Howie Hayes

The Sissy Series: Taboo Erotica Volume 1

Book 1 - A Sissy's Secret Desire: The Mistress, the Master and the Obedient Slave

Book 2 - Caught in the Act: A Sissies Secret Exposed

Book 3 - A Sissy in Training: Shaved and Submissive

Book 4 - His Secret is Out: Blackmail Never Felt So Good

Naughty Pleasures & Desires: Taboo Erotica Volume 3

Book 1 - Master and Slave: Two Wicked Sisters

Book 2 - Lessons from the Hired Help: Satisfaction is Black and White

Book 3 - Cuckolded by His Boss: When Fantasy becomes Reality

Book 4 - Afraid to Lose Him: Turning Her On, Calling Him Out

www.ingramcontent.com/pod-product-compliance
Lightning Source LLC
Chambersburg PA
CBHW071508030726
47593CB00003B/1213